This igloo book belongs to:

....

Contents

igloobooks

Published in 2013
by Igloo Books Ltd
Cottage Farm
Sywell
NN6 0BJ
www.igloobooks.com

OCE001 0613
2 4 6 8 10 9 7 5 3 1
ISBN: 978-1-78197-051-5

Printed and manufactured in China

Illustrated by Paul and Alice Sharp

Stories for

2

Year Old Girls

igloobooks

Lily's Lovely Garden

Lily is in her lovely garden. It is time to play outside.

She loves the leafy trees and her super-slippy slide.

Mommy pushes Lily's swing and she **swooshes** up so high.
Lily wants to touch the clouds and swish across the sky.

Mommy plants some pretty flowers in a neat and tidy row.
Lily helps to plant them, too. She can't wait for them to grow.

Lily pours on lots of water to give the flowers a drink.
They will grow up big and strong and be really bright and pink.

When Lily has finished watering, she runs off to explore.
She finds all sorts of insects, like spiders, ants and more.

"Hello," says Lily, when she finds a dotty Ladybug.
It is sitting on a leaf, looking happy, warm and snug.

Lily plays outside until it's nearly the end of the day.

She runs to tell her mother that the sun has gone away.

Mommy wraps Lily in a blanket and she curls up for a rest.
She can't wait to play outside again. Her garden is the best.

Rosie's Bedtime

Rosie is getting sleepy. She has had lots of fun today.
It is time to get ready to go to bed and put her toys away.

"Come on, Rosie," Mommy says. "Your bubble bath is ready. We can play with Yellow Duck and put pajamas on, like Teddy."

13

In the tub with Yellow Duck, Rosie has a soapy wash.
She pops the bubbles and splashes water with a giant **splosh**.

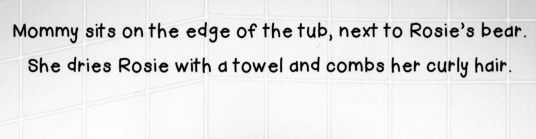

Mommy sits on the edge of the tub, next to Rosie's bear.

She dries Rosie with a towel and combs her curly hair.

Wrapped up in a towel, Rosie thinks she looks very funny.

Mommy says, "Here are your pajamas with a picture of a bunny."

16

Rosie wiggles into her pajamas and pulls the top over her head.
She grabs Teddy's little paw and jumps into her cosy bed.

17

Mommy reads a bedtime story from her special book.

Rosie loves the pictures. She makes sure Teddy has a look.

When Rosie is sleepy, Mommy kisses and hugs her tight.

"I love you lots, Mommy," says Rosie. "Night, night."

Cleo the Kitten

Cleo is my little black and white kitten. She is very bouncy
and very cute. She loves to run around and pounce
on wiggly bits of string.

I follow Cleo when she explores the garden. She leaps
between the flower bushes. She runs round and round,
chasing spiders and little butterflies. **21**

Sometimes, Cleo is a very naughty little kitten.

Mommy does not like it when Cleo climbs up the drapes.

Cleo is very good at hiding. Sometimes I can't find her anywhere, but she always comes back if I get her a tasty treat.

When I am painting pictures with my brushes and paint, Cleo likes to run across them and leave paw prints all over the floor.

Cleo knocks things over when she runs past tables and chairs,
but she is so cute that she gets away with everything.

Cleo loves it when I pour her a big saucer of milk.

She laps it all up, but she always wants more.

When I stroke Cleo's back, or rub her ears, she purrs and purrs.

I love Cleo very much. She really is the best kitten ever.

Clara's Cake

Mommy is making a special cake for someone.

"It will be a lovely surprise for them," says Mommy.

"Please can I help?" asks Clara.

"Yes," replies Mommy. She helps Clara put on a pretty, flowery apron. Then, she washes Clara's hands with warm, soapy water.

Mommy measures out all the ingredients that they will need.

Clara helps to tip everything into a big, pink mixing bowl.

"Now we need to mix everything together," says Mommy.

Clara stirs the mixture as fast as she can.

Then, Mommy pours it into a tin.

When the cake is in the oven, Clara and Mommy
make some pink and purple frosting.
The frosting is very sticky, but it tastes lovely!

Mommy takes the cake out of the oven and
lets Clara spread the frosting on.
Clara puts extra-tasty toppings all over it, too.

Mommy cuts two slices and makes a drink.

"Can you guess who the cake is for?" she asks.

"No," replies Clara.

"It's for me and you," says Mommy and Clara giggles.
Then, she and Mommy have a big slice each of their
best ever cake.

Hattie's Bath Time

Hattie loves getting messy. At breakfast, she splodges
porridge and milk down her clean t-shirt.
She gets jam all over her face.

Mommy says, "You look like you need a bath."

"No!" says Hattie, running out into the garden.

She thinks bath time is boring.

Hattie loves to play outside. In the garden, she can get really mucky. She squelches through the mud and crawls under leafy hedges.

When Hattie comes inside, she has mud splattered all over
her face and her top. She even has twigs in her hair.
Mommy says, "Now you really need a bath!"

"No!" says Hattie. She still does not want to have a bath.
She wants to go back outside and play with
the creepy-crawlies.

Mommy says she has a special surprise for Hattie.
"This is Mr Whale. You can play with him in
the tub," says Mommy.

Hattie thinks that Mr Whale is the best toy ever.
Mommy runs the taps and the tub fills up with foamy bubbles.
Some of the bubbles float up into the air and Hattie pops
them with her finger.

Hattie gets in the bath. She has lots of fun
playing with Mr Whale and Mommy, too.
"I love bath time!" says Hattie.

My Big Sister

I love my big sister because she is so much fun.

She pulls funny faces and tells silly jokes.

My sister likes to draw pretty flowers and butterflies.
Sometimes I draw a squiggly picture for her and she
says it is really good.

45

When my sister gets dressed up in a pretty dress, I do too.
She loves to wear lots of pink and gold and so do I!

My sister shows me how to put my hair
up in a pretty plaits, just like hers.
She puts flowers in my hair so that our hairstyles match.

I love my big sister because she gives soft, snuggly cuddles.
She loves to hug me tight. She is the best sister ever.